McBroom's Zoo

McBroom's Zoo

by Sid Fleischman

Illustrated by Kurt Werth

Published by
GROSSET & DUNLAP, INC.
A National General Company
New York

A
THISTLE
BOOK

Beasts and birds? Oh, I've heard some whoppers about the strange critters out here on the prairie. Why, just the other day a fellow told me he'd once owned a talking rattlesnake. It didn't *talk*, exactly. He said it shook its rattles in Morse code.

Well, there's not an ounce of fact in that. Gracious, no! That fellow had no regard for the truth. Everyone knows that a snake can't spell.

But yes, we did collect some mighty peculiar and surprising animals here on our wonderful one-acre farm. It's not generally known that we had the only Great Hidebehind in captivity. I must not forget to tell you about it.

If you've heard of me—Josh McBroom—you know that I'm a stickler for the honest facts. Why, I'd rather sit on a porcupine than tell a fib.

Of course, there are beasts and birds that come and go with the weather, so I'd best start with that ill-tempered spring morning. A low, ashy-looking cloud stretched from one horizon to the other, and the air was quiet. *Uncommonly* quiet. Not a note of birdsong to be heard. But I paid it no mind and we planted our farm in tomatoes.

I reckon you know about that astonishing rich topsoil of ours. My, it was a wonder! There was nothing you couldn't grow on our farm and quicker'n lickety-whoop. Why, just last Wednesday one of the young'uns left a hand trowel stuck in the ground and by morning it had grown into a shovel.

But to get back to those tomatoes. It wasn't five minutes before the vines were winding up the wood stakes and putting out yellow blossoms. Soon our one-acre farm was weighted down with green tomatoes. As they swelled up and reddened we had to work fast before the stakes took root.

"Will*jill*hester*chester*peter*polly*timtommary*larry*andlit-tle*clarinda!*" I called to the young'uns. "Time to harvest the crop. Looks like thirty tons, at least!"

"And look what's coming, Pa!" Little Clarinda shouted.

She pointed off toward the northwest and I about jumped out of my shoes. There appeared to be a stout black rope dangling from the clouds in the distance. "Tornado!" I yelled. "Into the storm cellar, my lambs! Run!"

The young'uns' dog, Zip, began to yip. We streaked it to the house, where my dear wife Melissa was taking a rhubarb pie out of the oven.

"Twister coming, Mama!" Polly cried out.

"And heading this way!" Will added, glancing out the window.

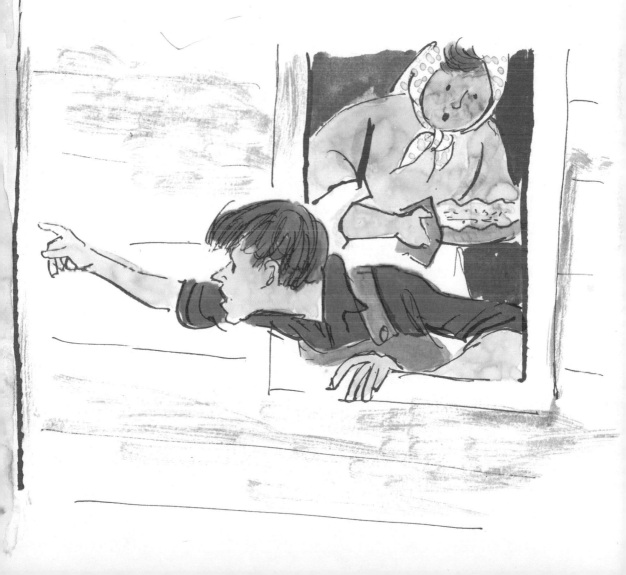

We all tumbled down into the storm cellar and shut the slanting doors after us. We could hear a whistling in the air as that twister drew closer. There was nothing to do now but wait it out in the darkness underground.

"Do you think it'll carry off the house?" Jill asked.

"And your Franklin automobile, Pa?" asked Chester.

Why, our farm's too trifling small for a whirlwind to go out of its way for," I said. "Nothing to worry about, my lambs."

But the whistling in the air became a screech and we knew that cyclone wasn't far off. The screech became a howl and we knew it was closer still. The howl became a roar and we knew that infernal twister was upon us!

The young'uns covered their ears. Mercy! The very earth shook. Overhead, we could hear the house windows explode. And for a last moment it seemed that all the air in the cellar was sucked up and away. At least, I believe that's what made our hair shoot up on end.

Then the roar faded to a howl, and the howl to a screech and the screech to a whistle. I was dead certain our house had gone up in sticks and the air-cooled Franklin automobile with it. I scampered up into the daylight.

"Glory be!" I shouted. "Come see for yourselves!"

The house was still standing. And the Franklin, too!

But our joy hardly lasted a moment. That infernal freak of nature had come so close it had plucked our entire crop of ripe red tomatoes, vines, stakes and all.

Worse than that—*it had sucked up our powerful rich topsoil*. Every glorious handful! We found ourselves gazing at a one-acre hole in the ground where our farm had been. You'd think that tricksy twister had paused a moment to scoop it out clean.

"Oh, Pa." My dear wife Melissa began to cry, and the girls joined in.

I set my jaws and strode toward the old Franklin. "Dry your tears, my loves," I said. "That whirlwind is bound to tucker itself out and drop our farm somewhere. I aim to race after it."

Well, the Franklin was still standing, but in no condition to race. Tarnation! that pesky tornado had sucked the air out of the tires.

"Will—fetch the tire pump," I said. "Not a moment to lose!"

The boys and I took turns pumping up the tires. We had hardly got started when Zip sniffed out something alive cowering under the car. Peter crawled underneath and dragged the creature out.

No. It wasn't the Great Prairie Hidebehind.

But it was a mighty odd beast—never saw anything like it before. It appeared to be a small mountain goat with the tail and ears of a large white-tailed jack rabbit—but that wasn't what made it odd. No, indeed, the surprising thing was its legs. The beast wasn't constructed to stand on level ground. The legs on one side were amazing short and the legs on the other were amazing long. The poor creature was a bit dazed—it must have fallen out of the tornado along the way.

We had got the last tire pumped up when the girls gave a shout. Polly had run into the house to find the natural history book and turned up a picture of that wrong-legged beast. "Pa, it's a Sidehill Gouger!" she said.

Oh, it was mighty rare, the book said. It lived on steep hillsides and needed those two long legs and two short legs to walk upright. Of course, it went round and round one way only—it would tumble over if it tried to go the other.

"Can we keep it, Pa?" the girls asked, one after the other.

"We don't have any steep hillsides around here," I reminded them, and jumped into the Franklin. Will and Chester jumped in, too. They wanted to go chasing after that cyclone with me.

Well, it wasn't hard to follow. Gracious, no! It had not only snatched up our tomatoes, but emptied a bin of onions and sucked up three barrels of cider vinegar I had set out to age. You could see that twister for miles, spinning away as red as ketchup.

In fact, it *was* ketchup. As we raced along we could see it squirting everything in its path—barns, windmills and a bald-headed fellow tacking up KEEP OUT signs who hadn't dodged out of the way fast enough. He said later it was the best tomato ketchup he had ever tasted, though it was a mite gritty. But he didn't mind that. Our topsoil in that ketchup tornado had grown hair on his head.

Well, we must have chased that whirlwind forty miles across the prairie. About the last thing it found to rip up was a stretch of barbed wire. Then it ran out of mischief, so to speak. It dropped our farm in a great red heap and wasted away to the small end of nothing.

When we reached our pile of topsoil we could hardly believe our eyes. That freak of nature had not only fenced it with tomato stakes and barbed wire—it had even tacked up the KEEP OUT signs.

"Pa, how'll we ever fetch it all home?" Chester asked.

I scratched my head. It looked like two hundred wagon loads, at least, sitting on someone else's land. We'd be lucky if they didn't charge storage. My, what a heap of money it would cost to haul that farm forty miles back where it came from!

"Boys," I said softly. "Might as well head back home. Looks like we're tornadoed out of business. Unless we can figure some way to raise a mighty sum of money."

Just then Will pricked up his ears. "Hear that, Pa? Sounds like a tin teakettle steaming away."

"There are no teakettles out here," I said.

"I hear it too," Chester said. "And *there* it is!"

Well, it wasn't a tin teakettle. It was a peculiar-looking bird wailing away inside the barbed wire fence. *Mighty* peculiar. For one thing, it wore its feet backwards.

No. It wasn't the Great Hairy Prairie Hidebehind.

The boys crawled through the barbed wire and fetched the sad creature. It was about the size of a small turkey, only larger, and the cyclone had plucked all its feathers. The most surprising feature was its beak. It was shaped like the spout of a teakettle, and everytime the bird made that teakettle-boiling sound—why, steam came pouring out.

I shook my head in amazement. "I declare if that twister hasn't flushed some mighty uncommon livestock out of hiding," I said.

"Can we take it home?" the boys asked.

I shook my head, and cranked the Franklin. "With all its feathers gone the poor thing's bound to expire."

Well, the boys packed that nameless bird in ketchupy topsoil mud and before we had driven three miles a new crop of feathers began to sprout! They were the color of green tea, except the tailfeathers. Those were sterling silver and shaped like teaspoons.

All the way back we saw dazed chickens and pigs and prairie dogs caught up by that howling twister and spun away far from home. But the boys had lost interest in common barnyard animals. They now fancied themselves rare game collectors.

We couldn't have been more than a mile from home when Will shouted, "There's something, Pa!"

The boys jumped out and started chasing a catfish through the dust.

Well, there's nothing uncommon about a catfish—but this one appeared to be swimming through the dust *backwards*. Making good time, too. Gave the boys a merry chase!

They did manage to corral the confused fish. They flopped him in the back seat, and we rushed on home to get him in a tub of water before it was too late. I reckoned the twister had whirlwinded him out of a creek somewhere.

But I was dead wrong. That ungrateful rascal leaped right out of the water back into the dust. It had a considerable *dislike* for water.

Turned out the boys had caught a genuine Desert Vamooser—very rare. It swims tail first to keep the dust out of its eyes.

And wasn't I surprised to see how that wrong-legged Sidehill Gouger had made himself right at home! There he was running around the sides of our one-acre hole in the ground, counterclockwise, happy as a squirrel, and pausing only to gouge out shallow and mysterious pockets.

The young'uns turned the Desert Vamooser loose in the bottom and I gathered the family together to break the bad news about our topsoil.

"Maybe another twister will come along and fetch it back," Polly said hopefully.

That wasn't likely, and Mama began dabbing at her eyes with her apron. "I must have left the teakettle boiling," she remarked suddenly.

Mercy! We had forgot that shy, spout-nosed, vapor-blowing creature in the back of the car, and it had got lonely. The young'uns crowded around and gazed at it in wonder.

"Look, Pa, its feet point behind it," Larry said.

Well, it didn't take long to discover what nature of bird the boys had found. It was a Silver-Tailed Teakettler—very rare. The book said no hunter had ever tracked one down to pluck its wonderful sterling silver tailfeathers.

And little wonder! I reckoned we knew something that wasn't in the book—those wrong-way feet. We let it out and saw that it left backward footprints. My, that was clever! Anyone following those tracks would proceed where the Teakettler had *been*, not where it was *going*.

"Pa," Little Clarinda blurted out. "We've got us a zoo. Our very own zoo! We could charge a penny."

"A nickel," Larry declared.

"A dime," Mary said.

"A quarter, at least," Tim insisted. "Didn't Pa say it will take a heap of cash money to fetch back the farm?"

A zoo! The thought near took my breath away. Wouldn't folks come from miles around to see these rare creatures? It wouldn't surprise me if we had the only Teakettler, Desert Vamooser and Sidehill Gouger in captivity.

"Glory be!" I exclaimed. "A zoo, did you say? Why, a zoo we'll have! No telling what other rare beasts that twister twisted up and scattered along the way. Not a moment to lose, my lambs!"

Well, the young'uns scurried after butterfly nets and gunny sacks to go collecting—all except Will. "Pa," he called, stooping at the rear of the Franklin. "Look at these tracks—coming all the way down the road. Far as the eye can see. I do believe something followed us home."

My, but they were outlandish paw prints! Clearly a two-legged beast that appeared to walk only on the tips of its toes. Toes? Why it had *seventeen* toes—eight on the left foot, nine on the right.

"We must have scared it off," I remarked, looking all about. And when the young'uns turned up ready to set out, I said, "Keep your eyes peeled for a seventeen-toed critter. That would be a fine catch for our zoo."

Well, the whole family spread out along the twisty path of the tornado. By early candlelight we returned home with several uncommon beasts and birds, including a rare Spotted Compass Cat—its tail always pointed north. But we'd seen neither hide nor hair of that two-legged, seventeen-toed visitor.

What we did see—standing at the very edge of our one-acre hole in the ground—was a two-legged, hairy-faced varmint that I recognized to be a man. He had a shotgun in one hand, a deer rifle in the other, a revolver in his belt and a large skinning knife between his teeth.

He was raising the rifle to his shoulder when I gave a shout. "What in tarnation do you think you're doing, sir! Who are you?"

The rifle exploded. "Tarnation yourself!" he shouted. That man could talk with the skinning knife between his teeth. "You made me miss! I want that Sidehill Gouger and mean to have him—stuffed and mounted. I'm a hunting man, that's who I am, and I've got a hunting license to prove it."

I was bristling mad. "Well, you're trespassing and you don't have a license for that. Furthermore and whatsmore, this is a zoo, sir, and you can't hunt in a zoo."

"A *zoo!*" he laughed. That man could even laugh with the skinning knife between his teeth. "I don't see any signs. Light's failing. I'll be back."

Of course, I stood guard all night long. The young'uns busied themselves making signs and we posted them all around our farm.

McBROOM'S ZOO
No Hunting Allowed!

Well, that fellow didn't show up at the crack of dawn. But a flock of sage hens did. They made nests in the hillside gouges the Sidehill Gouger had gouged out. I declare —those hens had been searching for him!

It turned out they weren't true sage hens. They were Galoopus Birds—very rare. Nesting in the steepest places, the Galoopus laid square eggs so they couldn't roll off down the slopes.

As the morning brightened I noticed there were more of those tiptoe tracks about—and very fresh.

"Jill," I said. "Is there anything in the natural history book about a seventeen-toed animal?"

She went to look it up while the other young'uns scampered off to post signs announcing the opening of our zoo. That flock of Galoopus Birds would be a fine addition, not to mention the critters we had brought back in gunny sacks the day before. The prize of the lot was a toothy, moose-headed Spitback Giascutus, and it did come in handy.

For just then that two-legged, hairy-faced hunting man turned up. I did wonder if he had seventeen toes, but he was wearing boots.

"You can see the signs," I snapped.

"Oh, I can see the signs," he chuckled between the skinning knife in his teeth. "But I can't read."

Quick as lightning he raised the rifle and fired. I thought sure he had bagged our Sidehill Gouger, but no, he had taken a sudden fancy to the moose-headed Giascutus. And that was a mistake. No one had *ever* been able to shoot a Spitback Giascutus.

What happened next was truly amazing! The Giascutus raised its antlers and caught the lead ball between its teeth. He spit it right back with remarkable aim and took a nick out of that infernal hunter's left ear.

Didn't he leave in a hurry, though! He'd never been shot at by an animal before. But I feared he'd be back.

McBroom's Zoo
No
Hunting Allowed

Jill came hurrying out of the house with the book. "Pa, the only seventeen-toed creature known is the Great Seventeen-Toed Hairy Prairie Hidebehind—and it's ex-extinct."

"Extinct?" I replied, thoughtfully. "Well, it may be extinct in the book, but there's one alive and lurking around here somewhere. And I declare if those don't look like fresh tracks just behind you."

I didn't mean to scare her—but she did jump back. Not that there was a creature to be seen. According to the book no one had *ever* laid eyes on a Hidebehind. It was always hiding behind something. Oh, it was slick at the game. A Hidebehind could be following you on its tiptoes, but it did no good to look. Every time you spun around it would still be hiding behind you!

Well, the news spread quickly that we had a dry-land fish that swam backwards and birds that laid square eggs. A few folks turned up, and then more folks and before long whole crowds of folks—some from out of state! The young'uns charged a quarter—kids free—and took turns lecturing on the surprising habits of our animals.

My, didn't we do a brisk business! Mama made barrels
of lemonade and I slept in the daytime so I could stand
watch at night. That hunter with all his guns was a worry.
And I did mean to have a look at the Great Seventeen-
Toed Hairy Prairie Hidebehind.

I tell you, it was a mite scary guarding the zoo at night.
I was certain that Hidebehind was following me about,
but every time I whirled around it whirled around too. I
even tried walking about with a hand mirror, but the Hidebehind was too eternal clever for tricks like that.

But one night when I whirled around I saw that ornery hunter sneaking down among the zoo animals. He barely got his rifle raised before the Teakettler steamed out a warning. The Desert Vamooser streaked backwards and threw a large fishtail full of dust into his eyes. Ruined his aim, of course—near blinded him for a month, it seemed.

By that time we had raised enough cash money to tote back our topsoil. Everyone agreed we had best turn the uncommon creatures back into the wild where they belonged. Of course, the young'uns hated to part with them. And I do believe the animals were happy with us. But there was the danger they would end up, one by one, on that two-legged varmint's wall—stuffed and mounted.

So the next morning we took down the zoo signs and loaded up the car with animals—mercy, there was hardly room for the young'uns!—and took off for the wildest parts of the prairie. We found a dusty old river bed for the Desert Vamooser, but it fell dark before we discovered a a sidehill for the Sidehill Gouger. We didn't rightly know what sort of country the Silver-Tailed Teakettler came from, but it began to steam happily as we ran through a patch of poison ivy and we dropped it off there.

Well, you might think we'd get lost chasing about in the middle of the night in the middle of nowhere—far from it. Didn't we have that Compass Cat with its tail always pointing due north? It was the last animal we turned loose.

Our farm? Oh, we got the topsoil hauled back—the wagons stretched out for half a mile and it took the better part of a week. But my thoughts were still on that Great Seventeen-Toed Hairy Prairie Hidebehind. Every morning I found fresh tracks. I *did* want to have a look at it. I began practicing whirling about—faster and faster.

Well, I got mighty fast. Before breakfast one morning I was out by the well and felt certain I was being followed. I whirled about quick as you please—and saw that backward-footed Silver-Tailed Teakettler. It had come back.

"Will *jill* hester *chester* peter *polly* tim *tom* mary *larry* and-little*clarinda*!" I called, and they came bounding outside.

"Looks like that fellow means to stay. You've got a new pet."

Well, they took the Teakettler inside the house—and just in time. Not a moment later that hairy-faced hunting man turned up armed to the teeth, as usual, and wearing goggles. He didn't mean to have dust thrown in his eyes again.

"You're too late," I said. "The animals are gone—every one."

"I see fresh tracks," he answered gleefully, lowering his nose to the ground like a bloodhound. "Reckon I'll follow them and bag myself that big bird."

He couldn't see too well with those goggles on. He over-
looked the Hidebehind's paw prints and went loping away
—following the Teakettler's backward tracks. As far as I
know he followed them right back where they started—a
hundred miles across the prairie in a patch of poison ivy.
We never saw him again.

But I did see the Great Seventeen-Toed Hairy Prairie Hidebehind! Indeed, I did! Not that I ever learned to whirl about fast enough—without help.

It was dusk and I sat down on a small wood stump to shake a rock out of my shoe—only it wasn't a small wood stump. It was a porcupine with its quills up. Didn't I jump! And didn't I whirl about *quick*!

Glory be! There he stood—the Great Seventeen-Toed Hairy Prairie Hidebehind!

Well, that shy beast was so embarrassed to be seen that he immediately hid behind *himself*. At least, I reckon that's what happened, for he just seemed to spin out of sight. A few tufts of orange hair settled to the earth like feathers.

We never saw his tracks around our wonderful one-acre farm again. But I'm certain he's still lurking about somewhere, hiding behind someone. Of course, he's quite harmless.

Mercy! He could be hiding behind YOU.